To Katlyon &
3 dorcey;

Worship is a reminder of
God's great love
for you!

In His grace & service
Suzanne Rom 1:5
2007

This book is presented with love to

from

Published by "Because We Care, Ministries"
A PA Registered Non-Profit Corporation
143 Mill Road, Schwenksville, PA 19473
www.woofi.org woofimissions@aol.com
IRS 501-C-3 Approved

ISBN 978-1-4243-1412-6

First Printing 2006

Written by: Suzanne Geiss

Illustrated by: Alan MacBain

Edited by: Melissa Geiss

Printed by: Printworks & Co, Inc.

Dedication

I give the praise, honor and glory to our Precious Lord for the inspiration of the Woofi story.

In loving memory of the late Pastor Bob "Woofi" Weaver who demonstrated his passionate love for the Lord, and love for his dear wife Jean, and showed us what it meant to have unconditional love, just like the Lord.

Forward

While on our way to Romania in 2003 on a mission's trip to visit needy and orphaned children, we took with us a little, plush puppy I had named Woofi, the Missionary Puppy. Not knowing how I was going to use Woofi, I sought the Lord's direction. While on the airplane, I began to pray, "Dear Lord, these precious children need to know you and your comfort. Lord, I ask that you would please bring to my mind a story of how I could share your comfort and love with them." After praying, immediately a story came to my mind. I could hardly write it down fast enough. I shared it with my husband and he asked me, "Where did you get that?" I said, "The Lord brought it to my mind." Without hesitation he said, "You need to tell the story to the children when we get to Romania."

The story became such an incredible blessing to all of us, as we watched the children being captivated as I shared the Woofi story. Then I realized that the Lord had not given me the story just for the needy children of Romania, but for all the children of the world, to encourage them to come to know Christ as their Savior and Lord of their life.

We are all challenged by God's word to share the gospel. God has given us the privilege and authority to tell everyone everywhere what God has done for them, so that they **will believe** and **obey** him, bringing **glory** to His name!

Our mission and goal is to share the good news with everyone and bring glory to His name. May you store up many treasures for heaven as you help us share God's message through the Woofi ministry!

Many blessings,
Suzanne and Woofi too!

Acknowledgements

This is the most difficult part to write. I pray I do not forget anyone as there have been so many who have helped and have been a tremendous encouragement and blessing along the way. I knew from the start that I could not write this book or start this ministry on my own, nor did God intend for me to do so. The Lord tells us, "Two people can accomplish more than twice as much as one."

I couldn't have written this book without my beloved husband and partner in the ministry, Rick. He is a constant help in so many ways.

Thank you to my precious children, Kevin and Michelle, their mates and my children in love, Melissa and Rich, and my cherished grandchildren, Rich, Lauren, Benjamin and Nathaniel, who have listened to this book and looked at the artwork until they all know it by heart. Thank you for your insights, encouragement, and unconditional love which have been invaluable blessings to me. May you all carry the torch for the Lord by being a continuing light to show the lost the way.

Many thanks to the following people who have helped to bring this ministry to light in more ways than can ever be imagined: Annette, Betty, Carolyn, Carrie-Anne, Downy, Elva, Fred, Lauren, Mary Kae, Marty, Nancy, Shannon and Pastors Bill, Kevin, John and Rick.

And a very special thank you to our incredible illustrator, Alan MacBain, who caught the Woofi vision immediately and worked patiently and diligently to bring this story life. May God continue to bless all of you.

Suzanne (Woofi's mom)

About the Illustrator

Alan MacBain is an award winning editorial cartoonist, freelance cartoonist and illustrator. His work has been seen on PBS, and he has illustrated for children's educational magazines including: "Humpty Dumpty," "Children's Digest" and "Jack and Jill."

In his words he says: "Creating and illustrating the characters for Woofi was a delightful experience."

The Missionary Puppy!

Written by Suzanne Geiss
(and inspired by the Lord)

Illustrated by Alan MacBain

Edited by Melissa Geiss

Hi! My name is "Woofi", and I would love to tell you the story of how I was given my name and became a missionary puppy.

My story begins in a big red barn where I lived with my mommy and five brothers and sisters. I was different from them all. They were black and white, but I was brown and white.

They were all so well behaved, but not me.

was full of **curiosity, spunk and adventure**, and it seemed like I was
always finding something to explore.

One day, I noticed a big shiny bucket that the farmer had left on the bench. I was curious to see what was inside. I jumped onto the bench and when I did, I accidentally tipped over the bucket. **CRASH! BOOM! BANG!** It fell onto the floor and milk splattered everywhere.

was so frightened that I scurried up the ladder to hide in the hayloft. I soon
realized that I couldn't get back down.

"WOOF! WOOF! WOOF!" I barked, crying out for help.

The farmer was milking the cows and heard me barking. He found me hiding up
in the hayloft.

"You sure are a curious little puppy," he told me. "I hope that your curiosity
doesn't get you into **BIG** trouble one day!"

As soon as he set me down on the floor, I scampered over to my mommy, and snuggled up close to her.

Feeling safe again, I fell sound asleep.

The next day when the farmer came into the barn to milk the cows, I noticed he had left the barn door open.

Quick as a wink, I scooted right out the door in search of a **new adventure**.

was so excited! I could hardly believe my eyes. Outside the barn I found a
hole new world to explore. I discovered a dirt road, and followed it eagerly.

As I was running down the dirt road I noticed a beautiful green meadow. There were butterflies, bumblebees and birds flying everywhere. They sure looked like they were having a grand old time. Lickety-split, I dashed over to join in the fun. I played in the meadow all day long and had a great time.

Soon I felt my belly growling, and I realized I was getting hungry. Even worse, I began to miss my mommy.

"WOOF! WOOF! WOOF!" I barked. **"I want to go home!"**

found the dirt road again, and ran as fast as I could, thinking that I was headed toward home.

All of a sudden I heard a loud rumble. A big, red farm truck zoomed by, throwing dust and dirt all over me.

I coughed and coughed and sneezed and sneezed, and I tried to rub the dust out of my eyes.

When the man in the truck saw me, he slammed on his brakes, and quickly backed up. He jumped out of the truck, picked me up by the scruff of my neck, and threw me onto the seat next to him.

was trembling with fear, but deep down inside, I hoped that the man was escuing me and taking me back home.

WOOF! WOOF! WOOF!" I barked, to thank him for picking me up.

Much to my surprise, the man did not take me back to my home. Instead, he took me back to his farm where he put me into a dirty dog pen, full of big, mean, ugly dogs. They were not one bit happy to see me.

They growled and snarled at me when I tried to get near their food. I was so terrified. I realized I had to find my way out of there.

Immediately, I began looking for a way to escape. I noticed a small hole under the fence on one side of the pen. I tried to squeeze through it, but I couldn't, so I began to dig. I **dug** and **dug**. I **dug** all through the night. Finally, at the crack of dawn, I saw that the hole was big enough for me to squeeze through.

Hot diggity dog! I did it! I was free at last.

I began running as fast as my little legs could carry me, looking for the dirt road that would lead me back to my mommy.

It seemed like I ran forever. My paws hurt. I was hungry and thirsty. I was frightened and I missed my mommy!

"WOOF! WOOF! WOOF!" I cried, "I have to find my way back home!"

As I came around a bend in the road, I saw a bridge. A little stream was flowing beneath the bridge, and I quickly ran over to it and began to drink.

was so thirsty, and the water was **lip-smacking** good.

rested for a little while, then set out again in search of my mommy.

crossed over the bridge and continued down the road. I was truly amazed when I found a busy street. I saw cars and trucks and tall buildings everywhere, but no big red barn.

s I explored one of the streets, I found a **beautiful park** where children
were playing.

quickly forgot about how lonely and hungry I was, and I hurried over to one of
he little girls who was playing in the park.

She took one look at me, scooped me up, and cuddled me in her arms. It was love at first sight.

She stroked my head ever so gently.
"Wow!" I thought. "This isn't my mommy, but it sure does feel **good**."

he little girl and I played together all day long. She even shared her picnic lunch
ith me.

was **paw-lickin'** good, and I barked to let her know I was thankful.

As the sun began to set, the little girl's father said, "It's time to go home now, Lauren. Say goodbye to the little puppy."

"Oh, no!" I thought. "I'll be all alone again. WOOF! WOOF! WOOF!" I barked with fear.

Lauren looked down at me, and I couldn't have felt more heartbroken, even if I had tried.

She then pleaded to her father, "Please, please, Daddy! Can't I take the little puppy home with me? Please?" Lauren's daddy looked around the park and noticed that everyone else was gone.

Well, O.K. We can take him home, but tomorrow we will have to put an ad in the newspaper to see if anyone has lost a puppy."

The little girl was so happy she squealed with delight. I was so thankful and excited that I jumped with joy. "WOOF! WOOF! WOOF!" I barked as she carried me home in her arms.

Lauren's daddy put an ad in the newspaper. Days went by, but no one called about a lost puppy.

Then one day, Lauren's daddy announced to the family, "It looks like we can keep the puppy, since no one has called to claim him."

I jumped up and down. I knew that I would not be hungry, lonely or lost anymore. I finally had a real home. I had someone to love, and somebody to love me.

"WOOF! WOOF! WOOF!" I barked joyously.

hen Lauren's daddy said to her, "Now that he is your puppy, you need to give im a name."

auren picked me up and looked at me, and said, "What should I name you, recious little puppy?"

responded with a "WOOF! WOOF! WOOF!"

know what I'll call you!" exclaimed Lauren. "**Woofi!** I'll call you Woofi!" I could ardly believe my ears! I had an awesome new home and a name that fit me erfectly: "WOOFI."

In my new home, I learned a great deal about my family. I realized how much they loved God, loved each other and how much they even loved me!

I listened very closely when I heard them talking about **Jesus**.

I was curious to learn more.

I heard Lauren's daddy tell her that Jesus has a great love for everyone, and that He wants each of us to be a part of His family.

But then her daddy explained how sin keeps us apart from God. "Sins," he said, "are anything you think, say, or do that displeases God. For example, you sin when you don't tell the truth or when you take something that doesn't belong to you. We all sin and deserve to be punished for our sins. That is why God had to send his son, Jesus, to take the punishment for our sins."

"Wow!" said Lauren.
"Jesus must really love me a lot to do that."

"Yes, Lauren, he does," her daddy said. "He died and rose again so that you could be a part of God's forever family. If you believe and accept what Jesus has done for you, you can become one of God's children too!"

Lauren then told her parents that she wanted to pray. She kneeled down and bowed her head and began to pray as I snuggled up close to her.

"Dear God, I know that I am a sinner, I am sorry for my sins. Please forgive me. I believe with all my heart Jesus took my punishment when he died and rose again. Thank you for forgiving me. I want you to be the Lord of my life. In Jesus' name, Amen."

I was overjoyed to hear her decision to follow Jesus.
"WOOF! WOOF! WOOF!" I barked.

few months later, the family decided to become missionaries and move Romania where they would be sharing the love of Jesus with the people the village of Dobresti (Dew-bresh).

Wow!" I thought. "Now I can become a missionary puppy and bring a hug and e message of God's great love to all the children of the world."

And that is exactly what I did! The Bible says, "Precious are the feet of those who bring the good news."

And I say, even if it's a puppy's feet!
WOOF, WOOF, WOOF!

Woofi's Family: Rich Jr., Rich, Michelle, Lauren, Rick (Woofi's dad), Woofi,
Suzanne (Woofi's mom), Benjamin, Kevin, Melissa & Nathaniel

Woofi would like to meet you!

For more information go to www.woofi.org